First published in the UK in 2017
by New Frontier Publishing Pty Ltd
93 Harbord Street, London SW6 6PN
www.newfrontierpublishing.co.uk

ISBN: 978-1-912076-63-5

A CIP catalogue record for this book is available from the British Library.

Designed by Celeste Hulme

Printed in China
10 9 8 7 6 5 4 3 2 1

Marvin and Marigold

THE BIG SNEEZE

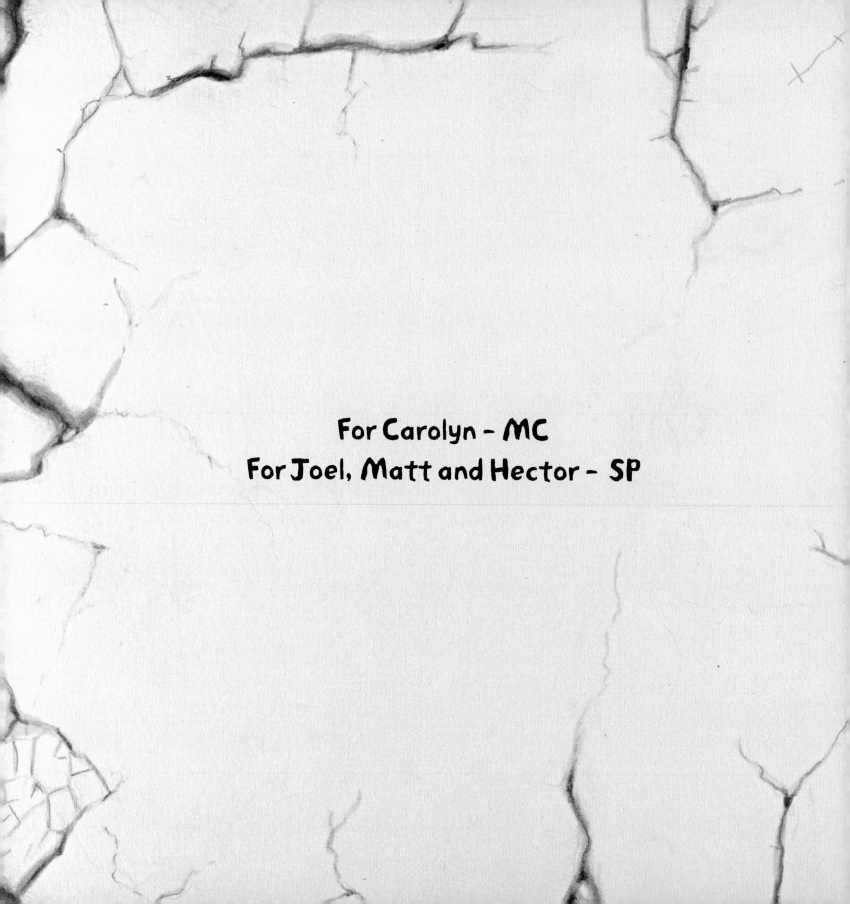

For Carolyn - MC
For Joel, Matt and Hector - SP

Marigold Mouse made a little mouse house
with some wool,
some felt and some bricks.

She built her house strong.
She built her house long –
with a bed made of feathers and sticks.

But Marigold's house was starting to crumble
for Marvin next door was making a rumble.

Whenever young Marvin smelled biscuits or cheese his whiskers would twitch ... and he'd let out a sneeze!

Ahh ... Ahh ... CHOO!

Now you may not know where the little mice go
when the sun sets over the town.
They seek treasures and cheese wherever they please
and roam all around, up and down.

Except for poor Marvin ... this wasn't for him –
his sneezes and snuffles created a din!

But through all the rumbles Marigold sang,
stacking her pans and pots.

She pranced and she danced her favourite dance
'til her little mouse legs had to STOP.

Then as Marigold rested to read a good book,
the whole of her house shuddered and shook.

Marvin let go of a gigantic sneeze –

'This simply won't do,' thought Marigold Mouse.
'I need a plan to save my poor house.'

So Marigold looked up a recipe book:

How to Cure Sneezes

By A. & G. Snook

Two pinches of salt,

black pepper and peas,

ginger and garlic

and old golden cheese

all mixed in a pot

will cure every sneeze!

But as Marigold stirred and stirred the pot more,
a letter arrived, placed under her door.

It was signed 'MM' and sealed with a paw.

'What could this be?' thought Marigold Mouse,
as she looked at the mess in her little mouse house.
She opened the letter and here's what it said:

Dear Marigold Mouse,

I'm sorry for all of the noise and the rumble
that's causing your house to shake and to crumble.
I'm leaving tomorrow and wish you the best.
I'm terribly sorry for being a pest.

Yours sincerely,
Marvin Mouse (MM)

'Oh dear,' thought Marigold, 'I know what to do!
It's time for poor Marvin to drink up this brew.'

So she poured out a cup of the old recipe
then set off with cheese, brown biscuits and tea.

When she opened the gate of Marvin the Mouse, a sign said:

'FOR SALE
One Little
Mouse House'.

As Marigold knocked on Marvin's front door,
some whiskers appeared ... a nose ... then a paw.

'Marvin,' said Marigold, quiet as can be.
'I've something to help you to stay next to me.'

'Drink this — it's for fixing the snuffily sneezes
that cause the big rumbles, tumbles and breezes.'
'Thank you,' sniffed Marvin, taking a sip
of the thick smelly brew, then biting his lip.

'Ooohhh!' Marvin gasped
and his mouse whiskers twitched.
They started to wibble and wobble and itch!

Then suddenly Marvin's whiskers went still.
He looked rather pale and was feeling quite ill.

'Try these,' said Marigold, beaming a smile.

She poured out some tea with biscuits and cheese,
Then waited to see if young Marvin would sneeze.

Ahh ...
Ahh ...

No sniffles.
No snuffles.
No rumbily breeze!

'**HOORAY!**' yelled Marvin.
'No more rumbles or tumbles
causing our houses to crack and to crumble.'

Then with tears in his eyes he hugged Marigold Mouse:
'Thank you for helping me stay in my house.'

'I'm glad I could help,' said Marigold Mouse.
'Come over for tea when I clean up my house.'

So Marigold packed up her teacups and plates
and headed for home

... after closing the gate.

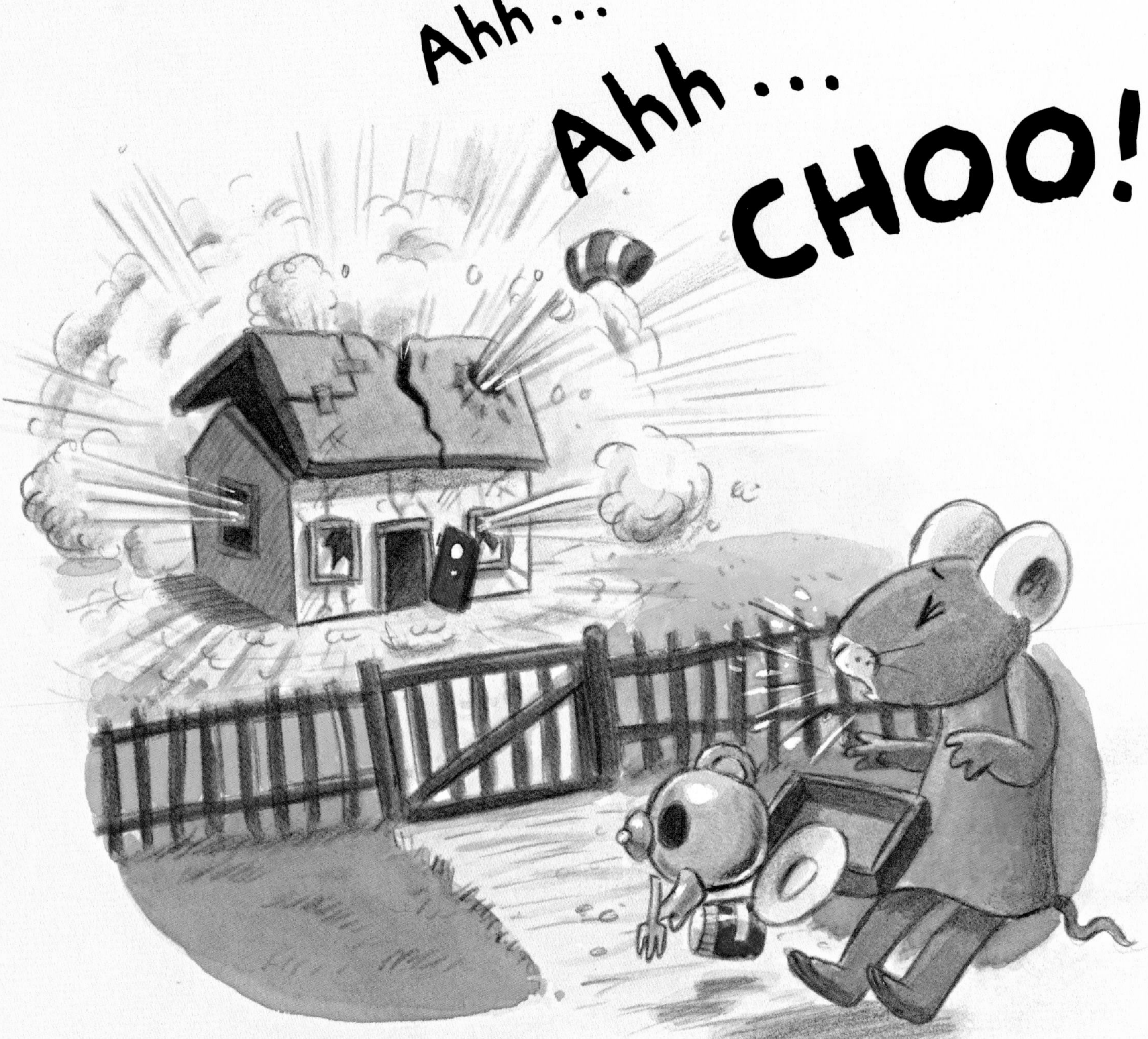
Ahh ...
Ahh ...
CHOO!